Pokémon
THE SERIES
SUN & MOON

Adventure on Treasure Island

THE SERIES

Adventure on Treasure Island

Adapted by Jeanette Lane

Scholastic Inc.

©2018 The Pokémon Company International. ©1997-2018 Nintendo, Creatures, GAME FREAK, TV Tokyo, ShoPro, JR Kikaku. TM, ® Nintendo.

Published by Scholastic Inc., *Publishers since 1920*. SCHOLASTIC and associated logos are trademarks and/or registered trademarks of Scholastic Inc.

The publisher does not have any control over and does not assume any responsibility for author or third-party websites or their content.

ISBN 978-1-338-23753-5

10 9 8 7 6 5 4 3 2 1   18 19 20 21 22

Printed in the U.S.A.   40
First printing 2018

CHAPTER 1

It was another beautiful, sunny day in the Alola region. Ash and Pikachu were enjoying their time on the tropical island of Melemele, which was covered in lush forests and golden beaches. There were all kinds of things to do—and so many new Pokémon to meet. Which was why our heroes were spending the day at . . . the mall?

"What's that?" Ash asked his friends from the Pokémon School. "Is it candy?"

Rotom Dex was always ready with an answer. The device knew nearly everything about Pokémon. "It's a kind of Pokémon food called Poké Beans," Rotom Dex explained.

The Poké Beans came in all sizes and colors. "Look, Steenee!" exclaimed Mallow, one of Ash's classmates. "Steenee likes these floral-patterned Poké Beans." Mallow's partner, Steenee, had recently evolved from Bounsweet.

The rest of Ash's classmates were there with their Pokémon, too: Lana, Sophocles, and Kiawe. Lillie had also joined them with her newly hatched Pokémon, Snowy. Snowy, with its bright blue eyes and thick, wavy, white tail, was an Alolan Vulpix.

"This Pikachu-colored one might be good," Ash said, picking up a mustard-yellow Poké Bean. "What do you think, buddy?"

"Pika, pika!" Pikachu approved of its best friend's choice.

While it was fun shopping for tasty treats, Ash wasn't so sure he wanted to join Mallow, Lana, and Lillie when they went to another store—in search of jewelry and other accessories. "The jewelry is made out of Heart Scales that wash up on the beach! And Corsola branches," Mallow explained. "Everything is amazing and completely natural!"

Kiawe, Sophocles, and Rotom Dex all thought of good excuses to head home, but Lana, Lillie, and Mallow convinced Ash and Pikachu to come with them.

Ash wasn't interested in the items inside the store, but outside the store was another story! He walked out the back door and onto a long balcony. It overlooked the ocean, which was a particularly bright blue that day with calm waves.

"Beautiful, isn't it?" came a voice from behind Ash.

When Ash turned around, he saw the manager of the store.

"It's wonderful to be able to look at the ocean while I'm at work," she said. "Can you make out that little island over there?"

"You bet!" Ash replied, eyeing the little island. He could see a sandy beach and tall palm trees.

"That's known as Treasure Island," the store manager explained. "I go there sometimes to find materials to make my jewelry. But I really do it for fun, because I get to see a lot of wild Pokémon."

Ash's jaw dropped. The wild Pokémon were one of the best parts of the Alola region. Ash's goal was to become a Pokémon Master, and he had learned a great deal since coming to the tropical islands. Observing Pokémon in nature was fascinating!

"I want to go to Treasure Island, too!" Ash declared. He looked at his partner. "What do you say?"

"Pika, pika!" As usual, Pikachu agreed with its Trainer.

"You're welcome to borrow my kayak if you'd like," the manager said.

"Kayak? Really?" Ash could hardly believe his good fortune!

"Of course," the manager responded. "I'll lend it to you as my little gift."

After a quick good-bye to Lana, Lillie, and Mallow, Ash and Pikachu set off across the bay. Each thrust of the paddle propelled them closer to the small island on the horizon.

"Ocean to the right . . . ocean to the left," Ash said, pausing to take a deep breath of salty sea air. "Ocean everywhere!"

Pikachu breathed in, too.

"The sky's almost as blue as the ocean!" Ash listened to the gentle waves on the side of the

thin boat. "It almost feels like we're the only ones on the planet. Weird, but awesome!"

After a peaceful moment, Ash was ready for action again. "We're almost there. Let's step on the gas!"

Using all his strength, he tugged the paddle through the water, one side and then the other. Water-type Pokémon rested on the rocks, taking in the sun. Others swam in schools around the kayak.

Soon, the boat's pointed bow ran into the soft, wet sand at the edge of the beach. Ash jumped out and pulled the boat from the water. "We made it!" he yelled to Pikachu.

They'd reached Treasure Island!

CHAPTER 2

Ash and Pikachu dashed down the beach. They couldn't wait to explore! The Trainer and his best pal were so excited, they nearly ran into a pack of Crabrawler.

"What's going on?" Ash mumbled, peeking over a pile of rocks at the Pokémon. The Fighting-type Pokémon were crowded around two Crabrawler that were battling. One raised its mighty claw and used Iron Fist. The other flew through the air and skidded across the hot sand.

"I think they're having a boxing match!" Ash told Pikachu. He popped his head over the rocks and called to the Pokémon. "That was an amazing punch! Mind if we hang out and watch?"

The group of Pokémon turned around and stared at Ash and Pikachu. Then they screeched in surprise and scurried off in the other direction.

"Aw, man!" Ash exclaimed. Were all the wild Pokémon on Treasure Island so shy?

Soon, Ash and Pikachu were distracted by another Pokémon—a Cutiefly. The tiny Bug- and Fairy-type Pokémon buzzed around Pikachu's head and landed on its nose.

"Hey, maybe it thinks you're a flower," Ash said with a laugh. When the Cutiefly whizzed away, Ash wanted to follow it.

The Pokémon led them down a path with tall, leafy trees on both sides. The path opened to a gigantic meadow. Hundreds of the small, winged Pokémon flitted around a field of colorful wildflowers.

Ash and Pikachu ran into the meadow with their arms wide. A small flock of Cutiefly placed a flower necklace over Ash's head.

"How cool is this?" Ash exclaimed. "It's just like paradise!"

"Pika-chu!" Ash's companion was just as delighted as he was. The beauty of nature was everywhere.

A line of Alolan Exeggutor walked along a trail through the flowery field. The long-necked Coconut Pokémon chanted in tune as they marched together. *"Exeggutor, Exeggutor, Exeggutor."*

Ash couldn't help but join in. He tagged along at the end of the Exeggutor line, lifting his knees high with each step. Pikachu was perched on his head.

Ash grabbed a leafy twig and waved it in the air as he repeated the chant with the Grass- and Dragon-type Pokémon. They didn't seem to notice him until Ash started to sing off-key. "Exeggutor!" he belted with a high, squeaky pitch.

At once, all the Exeggutor turned to Ash. They thrust their long necks at him; each neck had three coconut-shaped heads at the top. None of the heads were happy. They scowled and bared their pointy fangs.

Ash shrunk away a little. "Exeggutor?" he sang nervously, hoping to find the right notes.

The lead Exeggutor nodded. It seemed to accept Ash's improved melody. When it turned around and started walking again, the other Exeggutor followed. So did Ash. They ended up at a crystal-clear watering hole.

The Exeggutor all dunked their heads into the water, taking in big gulps. Ash and Pikachu did the same. They were thirsty! Then the giant Pokémon stepped into the water and started to wash off, making playful fountains with their many mouths.

Ash decided to swim, too! The Exeggutor let Ash and Pikachu climb their necks, and then the giant Pokémon would toss them into the water. What could be more fun than a Pokémon water park?

After a while, all the Exeggutor left the watering hole. "Thank you, Exeggutor!" Ash called as they ambled away.

Next, Ash and Pikachu headed to the beach to dry off. There they ate some Poké Beans, talked about the wonders of the Alola Islands, and dozed off in the heat of the sun.

The two friends napped peacefully for a while. They were tired from the exercise and the sun's strong rays.

When they woke up, they were not alone. Ash and Pikachu were surrounded by purple-and-silver Pokémon with shells on their backs and long, spiky tails. The Pokémon were chatting and giving off a constant hum.

"Oh, man . . ." Ash murmured. "What are they, anyway?!"

The Pokémon kept humming as they moved in closer, crowding close to Ash and Pikachu.

"What do they want with us?" Ash cried. He jumped up on a log. Pikachu leaped up and clung to Ash. Nervous sweat rolled down their faces.

Then one of the creepy-crawly Pokémon chomped down on Ash's foot. "Knock it off!" Ash screeched, shaking his leg. Several of the other Pokémon dove face-first into Ash's backpack. One came out with the bag of Poké Beans clenched in its jaws.

"Hey, that's ours!" Ash yelled. It was the only food he and Pikachu had!

The swarm of Pokémon scrambled down the beach. Pikachu took off after them.

The Pokémon neared the edge of the rocky shore. They were all going to dive off a cliff into the ocean, but Pikachu tackled the one with the bag of Poké Beans. The two Pokémon rolled toward the edge of the ocean, but Pikachu snatched the bag back just in time.

"Way to go!" Ash cheered.

Pikachu hopped up on his shoulder, and the two watched as the unknown, spiky-tailed Pokémon swam away.

"*Pika, pika,*" Pikachu murmured in Ash's ear.

"I've never seen those Pokémon either," Ash admitted. He took a deep breath of the ocean air and noticed that the sun had gotten much lower in the sky. "We'd better head back home."

They still had a long trip ahead of them.

CHAPTER 3

Before Ash and Pikachu could return to the kayak, they heard an unusual sound. It sounded like someone—or something—was in trouble.

"What's that noise? Where's it coming from?" Ash asked.

"Pika?" Pikachu's ears drooped with concern. *"Pikachu?"*

Ash wandered around the beach, listening closely. Pikachu stayed perched on his shoulder, its ears at attention.

But they could not figure out where the sound was coming from. On one side of them was the ocean; on the other was a tall cliff. In the middle was a sandy beach. They looked everywhere, but there was nothing that could be making the bubbling, squeaking, snuffling sound.

Pikachu scampered up a ledge of rocks. *"Pika, pika!"* It crept into a crevice in the cliff wall.

Pikachu sniffed. *"Pikaaa!"* It wanted Ash to look, too.

"In there?" Ash asked. "Yeah, you're right! I hear something in there."

But when Ash ducked down to look in the bottom of the crevice, he couldn't see a thing. It was dark, and the crevice seemed very deep. He shuffled closer and squinted, trying to see into the darkness.

Pikachu had its head buried in the crevice, too. It pushed and wiggled, trying to force its way inside.

"Hey, I remember that Pokémon," Ash said, finally catching a glimpse of purple and silver. It was one of the Pokémon with the plated shells they'd seen earlier on the beach. "It probably got lost, and now it's stuck and can't get out."

Ash stepped away. The cliff in front of him was almost a solid wall of rock that went straight up. "I wonder how the Pokémon got in there." Ash scowled, tilting his head back. "We've got to get it out, so I guess I have to climb that."

Ash turned his hat around, found a foothold, and started climbing. He searched with his hands for places to grab on and pull himself up. He made it almost halfway up the cliff, but then he lost hold and fell—on his back. *Ouch!*

Ash shook himself off and started climbing again, even more determined. "Oh, yeah? You can't beat me!" he yelled at the cliff. He peeked in the crevice again. "I promise, I'll get you out of there, so don't you worry."

Pikachu was not so sure. As Ash tried to climb the wall once more, his partner ran off down the beach.

"Hey, Pikachu! Where are you going?" Ash called, but Pikachu kept running farther down the beach.

"*Pika, pika, pika!*" it called.

Ash made it about as far as before, but then he fell flat again. His arms and legs were covered with scratches. His back pounded with pain.

It wasn't long before he heard a familiar chant. "*Exeggutor, Exeggutor.*"

"*Pika-chu!*" Pikachu cheered with excitement.

"Exeggutor?" Ash wondered aloud as he watched the long-necked Pokémon approach. Pikachu was holding on tight on top of one of

Exeggutor's heads. "But, Pikachu? Why?" Ash asked, feeling confused. "What's going on?"

As Exeggutor came closer, Ash began to understand Pikachu's plan. Exeggutor was so tall that its heads reached the top of the cliff! "I see," Ash finally admitted. "Great idea! You're a genius, Pikachu!"

"Here's the deal," Ash told Exeggutor. "There's a Pokémon stuck inside that rock! Give me a lift, okay?"

Ash grabbed on to the Pokémon's neck and shinnied up. Exeggutor easily lifted him and

Pikachu from the beach level to the top of the rock wall that overlooked the ocean.

"All right!" Ash yelled, hopping off. "Thanks, Exeggutor!"

Ash rushed over to the cliff's edge. There, he saw an opening to a cave-like area below. He could just make out the trapped Pokémon in the shadows. "I'm coming down," he called out. "You just relax, okay?"

Ash slipped between the two walls of rock, trying to lower himself slowly. Pikachu sat on his shoulder and held on with all its might. When Ash got to the place where the cave ceiling opened up, he had to leap into the sand. It was a long drop, and he landed with a loud *thud*.

The trapped Pokémon skittered away with a squeal. It ran headfirst into a bunch of rocks. It kept butting its head against them.

"I know," Ash said in a kind voice. He suspected the Pokémon was afraid. "It's scary, but you've got to stay calm." When he stepped toward the Pokémon, it scrambled away.

"What do you know?" Ash said, examining where the Pokémon had been hitting its head. A large rock blocked a crack in the cave wall. "So this is how you got in. But the rock is in the way now, and you can't get out." A loose pebble fell from above. "You're lucky you didn't get squished. Don't worry."

Ash bent down and pulled the rock with all his might, but he couldn't move it. He tried again, but the rock didn't budge.

"Hey, Pikachu! Help me out!" he said.

Pikachu bounded over to him. "Use your Iron Tail on that rock!" Ash called.

"Pika, pika!" Pikachu leaped in the air, its tail glowing with power. With a powerful swing of its zigzag tail, Pikachu attacked. The rock exploded into a cloud of powdery dust.

"Man, that was great!" Ash exclaimed. "Now you can get out of here," he told the trapped Pokémon.

"Exeggutor!" Even the Alolan Exeggutor sounded happy when it looked in the new, much bigger entrance to the cave.

"Okay, you can go," Ash said. "I'm sure your friends are worried about you." They all walked out of the cave and down the beach toward the ocean.

"Look at that," Ash said, pointing to a group of

Pokémon floating on the surface of the water. "They're your friends, right?"

The Pokémon dashed into the water, but then turned around and waddled back out. It made a grateful, cooing sound.

"Yeah?" Ash asked.

The Pokémon turned around and paddled its way to its friends. "Bye! Take care!" Ash called.

After they had swum out of eyesight, another Pokémon caught Ash's eye. This one was flying through the air in graceful swoops.

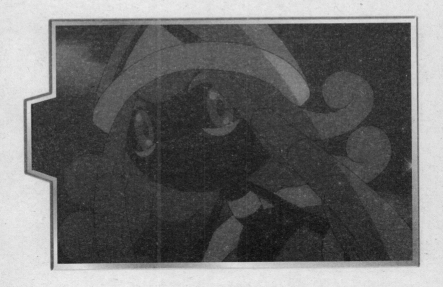

"Huh? A Pokémon?" Ash did not recognize this Pokémon, either. He did, however, notice that it had black markings similar to Tapu Koko. Ash's jaw dropped in wonder.

As the Pokémon swirled through the sky, a colorful glitter seemed to sparkle all around it. Some of the glitter rained down on Ash, disappearing as soon as it touched him.

Ash looked down at his arms. "The scratches . . . but how?" As the glitter touched his skin, all his cuts and scrapes disappeared.

"They're all gone. That was great! Thanks so much!"

He and Pikachu waved as the magical Pokémon flew out of sight.

It was the end of another amazing adventure for our heroes, but they still needed to get back to Melemele in the kayak. This time, they would be paddling under the stars. And who knew what excitement tomorrow might bring?

CHAPTER 4

Back at Professor Kukui's bungalow, Ash told his teacher all the details about the day on Treasure Island. He mentioned the beautiful meadow with all the tiny, flying Pokémon. He laughed as he retold the story of his dip in the swimming hole with the Exeggutor. But Professor Kukui was especially interested in one of Ash's stories—the one about the Pokémon he saw in the sky after he'd helped the trapped Pokémon escape.

"It was probably Tapu Lele!" the professor said.

"Tapu Lele?" Ash repeated. "Whoa." Even the Pokémon's name sounded cool. "Does the name mean it's Tapu Koko's friend?"

"Correct!" answered Professor Kukui.

"Meeting it is exceptionally rare! And the Pokémon you helped is most likely a Wimpod."

"Wow," Ash responded. "Wimpod?" He was excited to learn more about new Pokémon. He turned to Rotom Dex. "Will you check them out for me?"

"It's my pleasure!" answered Rotom Dex. "Tapu Lele. The Land Spirit Pokémon. A Psychic-Fairy-type. Tapu Lele playfully flutters around while scattering its mysteriously glowing

scales." Rotom Dex paused, floating in the air near Ash. "It is said whoever touches its scales is instantly healed."

Ash held out his arms and examined them again. "That's why my scratches are gone," he told the others.

Next, Rotom Dex switched screens. "Wimpod," it said. "The Turn Tail Pokémon. A Bug-Water-type. From beaches to seabeds, Wimpod live in all kinds of places. They eat anything, even if it's rotten. They're nature's vacuum cleaners!"

Ash nodded, taking it all in.

"You see, Tapu Lele is the Island Guardian of Akala Island. And meeting it was a stroke of luck!" said Professor Kukui.

"Yeah, I wanna see it again! Think I can?" Ash asked.

"If your luck holds out," his professor answered honestly.

"Nah, I don't need luck. No way! I'll see it again. We'll see it again!" Ash looked around at his friends. He felt very confident. He wanted to share his excitement with everyone—Pikachu, Rowlet, Rotom Dex, Rockruff. "You guys can all meet it, okay?"

On days like these, Ash felt like there wasn't anything he couldn't do.

Of course, things did not always go as planned. The very next morning, he found himself facing a new challenge.

Ash had gone to the market with Pikachu, Rockruff, and Rotom Dex. As usual, he had bought too much stuff and was having a hard time carrying it all. As he juggled the bags, a doughnut tumbled out and rolled over to the shop's owner.

"Alola, young man!" she said. "Out on errands?"

Ash knew her! She was friends with Litten. "Yes," he replied with a smile.

"This is yours," she said, holding out the doughnut.

Ash reached over to take it. Out of nowhere, Litten sprang up and snatched the doughnut away! It was just like old times. Litten was up to its usual tricks!

"Litten! How are you?" Ash was not upset that Litten stole the food. In fact, he was happy to see the pesky little Pokémon again.

Litten, however, did not seem as pleased to

see Ash again. Instead of mewing a hello, it dashed off without a sound.

Ash and the others took off, too, hoping to track down the Pokémon.

Litten was as swift as always. It bounded through a crowd in the town square and went down cobblestone alleys. Ash and his team would not give up! But as they came to a bridge, Litten was nowhere to be seen.

"What? Where?" Ash gasped, trying to catch his breath.

"Pika! Pika! Pika!" Pikachu was pointing over the side of the bridge.

"What is it, Pikachu?" Ash asked, looking down. He saw a flight of steps leading to a lower level. There was a stone walkway that went along the side of the canal.

"Pika, pika!" Pikachu replied, pointing.

That's when Ash noticed Litten, leaping down the last steps.

"Look at that! So that's where Litten went," Ash declared.

"I can see Stoutland as well!" Rotom Dex announced.

Ash was not surprised to see that Litten and the much older Stoutland were still sticking together. The two Pokémon were pretty much inseparable. Litten immediately set the doughnut on the sofa where Stoutland was resting. Stoutland gobbled it up gratefully.

As soon as Stoutland was done, Litten trotted toward an old stump on the walkway. The Pokémon took a battle stance and placed its four legs evenly. Litten leaned forward with its tail in the air. It was ready for a practice battle!

Before Litten could start its attack, Stoutland interrupted it. While still stretched out on the sofa, Stoutland arched its back. A bright red flame appeared along its spine. Then it grunted and sprang upward.

"I've seen that move before!" Ash exclaimed.

"It's using Fire Fang!" Rotom Dex announced, sounding just as thrilled as Ash.

As Stoutland soared through the air, orange

fire appeared to fill its mouth. Stoutland landed on the walkway and clenched the stump in its teeth. Brilliant orange flames roared from its mouth. With a blast of smoke, the stump was gone.

Stoutland very slowly made its way back to the sofa. Exhausted, it sighed and collapsed on the cushions.

Litten went back to its place on the walkway. This time, it took its battle position in front of a giant tree.

"Stoutland, stout," Stoutland grumbled, giving the younger Pokémon advice.

Litten took its stance and pounced. Fire burst from Litten's mouth, just as it had from Stoutland's. A red glow surrounded Litten. As the Pokémon came in for a landing, it latched its fangs on the tree.

But . . . nothing else happened. The flames died down, and Litten landed—*splat*—on the walkway.

CHAPTER 5

After watching Stoutland complete a Fire Fang attack—and Litten try but not quite succeed—Ash and his team hurried down the stairs to the canal below. Ash wanted to check on the two Pokémon before Litten had a chance to rush off again.

"Hey, Stoutland," Ash said as he approached the elderly Pokémon. "How are you?"

Stoutland gave Ash a long look, and Litten grumbled. Litten seemed surprised that Ash and the others had found them. But Ash and Litten had a history. Litten should have known that Ash wouldn't give up that easily. He was genuinely concerned about the Fire Cat Pokémon.

"So, Litten," Ash began, "I guess you're practicing Fire Fang, aren't you?"

But a loud series of coughs from Stoutland drew Ash's attention back to the Big-Hearted Pokémon. "Stoutland?" Ash asked. "Are you all right?"

Pikachu and Rockruff looked concerned, too.

"Stoutland, stout." It was clear that Stoutland did not want anyone to worry. It wanted to be as independent as Litten! Maybe that's why the two got along so well.

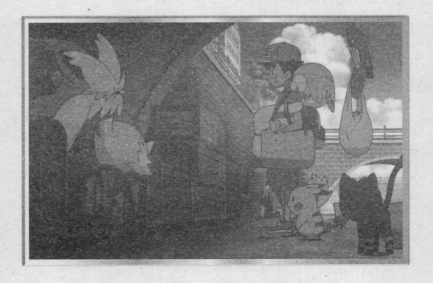

"Oh, yeah!" Ash said, searching through one of his bags. "I just bought some Berries. See? How about we split them?"

Before Ash could find the Berries, Litten zapped him with an Ember move.

"Yee-owch!" Ash cried, his face burning with Litten's surprise attack. Ash rushed over to dunk his face in the water of the canal.

Stoutland scolded its young friend. After all, Ash was just trying to be nice.

Ash looked up from where he was bent over the canal. Water was streaming down his face. "Litten hasn't changed a bit, huh?"

Litten did not look sorry. It looked like it was more determined than ever to master its new, more difficult move—Fire Fang.

Ash and the others agreed it was time to call it a day, so they headed back to Professor Kukui's. There, they talked about their meeting with Stoutland and Litten while they put away the food from the market.

Professor Kukui was fascinated by the special relationship between Stoutland and Litten. Rotom Dex shared a video that it had recorded. The video showed the two Pokémon working on their Fire Fang technique.

"That is rare," Ash's teacher declared. "You almost never see Pokémon of two different types practicing moves together." He leaned closer to Rotom Dex's screen. "See that? Their backs are both rounded. This is what they do to build up their energy."

"Yeah," responded Ash. "Come to think of it, they did that a lot."

"Pika," Pikachu agreed with Ash.

"That Stoutland is taking awfully good care of that Litten, all right," Professor Kukui said.

Ash agreed with the professor, but he also believed that Litten was taking good care of Stoutland.

*   *   *

40

The next day, Ash and Pikachu were walking home from the Pokémon School. As usual, Rotom Dex hovered next to them.

"I think we should go back and see Litten again soon," said Ash. "We can take some Berries."

"Pikachu!" Pikachu thought it was a great idea, yet Rotom Dex looked wary. Would Litten and Stoutland be happy to see Ash and his crew?

Before there was any time to think about it, Team Rocket—Ash's longtime enemies—stepped right into their path.

"What do *you* want?" Ash asked, putting his hands on his hips.

Jessie flipped her long, pink hair. "Prepare for trouble," she announced. "You're such a twerp bore."

"And then make it double," James chimed in. "I couldn't agree more!"

Team Rocket loved making a dramatic entrance.

"Team Rocket," Jessie and James declared. "Let's fight!"

"That's right!" cried Meowth, their Pokémon partner.

"Wobbuffet!" Another of Team Rocket's Pokémon, Wobbuffet, always agreed with Jessie, James, and Meowth.

Suddenly, a fire ball surrounded Team Rocket. They yelped in surprise, and Litten appeared. It bounded up to Ash and the others.

"Pika, pika?" Pikachu was instantly worried.

Litten stopped at Ash's feet and called out to him, its yellow eyes big with concern.

"It doesn't sound good," Ash admitted.

"Stop!" Jessie cried, annoyed.

"Interrupting is rude!" James added.

"That's the grub-grabber," Meowth realized, recognizing Litten. It had stolen Team Rocket's food in the past.

Ash had no time for Team Rocket's silly threats. "Pikachu, use Electro Ball!" he directed.

Pikachu jumped up and shot an Electro Ball at Team Rocket. Then it raced off with Ash and the others. They needed to see why Litten was so worried.

Team Rocket was offended. They had hoped for a good, fun fight. "Let's retreat and regroup," James suggested.

"Meowth, come along," Jessie called.

But Meowth wasn't thinking about the fight. He had something else on his mind. "No, thanks," Meowth replied. "I'm going to deal with this."

CHAPTER 6

Stoutland!" Ash called as soon as he spotted Stoutland. It was sprawled out on the walkway under the bridge of the canal, and something was not right. It was clear the Big-Hearted Pokémon was in distress.

"It's having trouble breathing!" Rotom Dex observed.

"This is what you were so worried about, right?" Ash confirmed with Litten.

"Ra-raow." Litten looked Ash right in the eye.

"Don't worry! We'll get Stoutland to a Pokémon Center right away!" Ash sounded very sure of himself as he bent down to lift Stoutland onto his back.

"You're going to carry it?" Rotom Dex asked.

"What else can I do?" Ash replied, grunting under the Pokémon's weight. "Stoutland's not heavy."

Ash hunched forward, draping Stoutland's enormous front paws over his shoulders.

"Pika, pika," Pikachu put in.

"But it's still big," Ash admitted. He was determined not to let Litten down. "Don't worry, Litten!" he said, moving toward the stairs. "Stoutland will be better in no time."

The group was so concerned that they did

not even realize they had passed Meowth as they left the canal walkway. The Scratch Cat Pokémon watched them go. Then he followed them.

Ash kept his promise to Litten. Soon they'd reached a Pokémon Center. The workers there helped Stoutland into a room right away. They used special machines to check on the Pokémon's heart and breathing.

Litten was not permitted to go into the room with Stoutland during Nurse Joy's exam. The Fire Cat Pokémon watched everything through a large window. Ash, Pikachu, and Rotom Dex waited right by Litten's side.

As soon as the doors opened and Nurse Joy came out to speak to Ash, Litten slipped inside. It jumped up on the exam table and began licking its friend's face.

"Hi, Nurse Joy," Ash said. "Is Stoutland going to be all right?"

Nurse Joy paused. "Stoutland isn't hurt, and it doesn't have any serious illnesses," she tried to explain. "It's just . . ." Nurse Joy paused again, searching for the right words. "Well, Stoutland is . . ."

Ash realized what Nurse Joy was trying to say. Ash had known that Stoutland was much older than Litten, but he wasn't sure exactly how old Stoutland was. "Do you think Litten knows?" he asked Nurse Joy.

"I think Litten can sense the truth," she responded, looking back into the exam room at the two Pokémon.

Ash took a deep breath. He wondered what it would mean for Litten. He wondered if he could do anything for its friend.

A little while later, Ash called Professor Kukui to ask permission to stay at the Pokémon Center overnight. That way, he could watch over Stoutland and Litten.

"I agree," Professor Kukui said. "You should stay with Stoutland tonight."

"Thank you, Professor," Ash replied with relief.

"It's obvious Litten thinks you're a human it can trust," Professor Kukui added. He sounded proud of his student. "Otherwise, it never would have come to you for help like that. Do what you can."

"Right," Ash answered.

After he hung up, Ash hurried to the market. Litten and Stoutland would need food for dinner. He decided that he, Rotom Dex, and Pikachu would buy the most delicious-looking Berries they could find. That might help Stoutland and Litten feel better!

As soon as Ash and his Pokémon returned, they headed for Stoutland's exam room. "Check out the Berries I brought for you two," he announced as he opened the door.

But the exam room was empty. Stoutland and Litten were gone!

"Oh no, it can't be!" Rotom Dex cried. "Considering Stoutland's condition, they couldn't have gone far."

"I know where they went," Ash said, dropping his bag and rushing for the door. "Let's go!"

"*Pika!*" Pikachu agreed.

The three friends rushed out and headed down a narrow street. At once, a dark figure appeared in front of them. They skidded to a stop.

"It's Meowth," Ash said.

The Pokémon stood his ground, squinting at them.

"Hey, what do you want?" Ash asked. He didn't have time for a one-on-one battle with Meowth!

"I've got a bone to pick with the two of you," Meowth replied. "Litten's the kind of Pokémon that never gives up. So you twerps better make sure you never give up on Litten, got it?"

"What are you talking about?" Ash asked.

"I'm done," Meowth declared. "Don't forget it!" Then he dashed off without another word.

"Man, that was weird," Ash said. Pikachu and Rotom Dex agreed.

But they were glad to hear Meowth was looking out for Litten, too. They vowed to stay true to the Fire Cat Pokémon. They would not give up on Litten.

CHAPTER 7

Ash and his friends were not going to give up on Litten . . . or Stoutland. Still, Ash decided to let the two Pokémon have some time alone. Ash had taken Stoutland to the Pokémon Center. He had done all he could do to help. For now, Ash and the others went back to Professor Kukui's house.

The next day was cloudy. Ash, Professor Kukui, and their Pokémon friends headed out for the canal. They were going to check on Litten and Stoutland.

By the time they arrived, it was raining.

"Litten!" Ash called as soon as he saw Litten. It was sitting in the rain, crying. And it was all alone.

"Professor, where's Stoutland?" Rotom Dex asked.

"I'm sorry," the professor responded sadly.

Litten walked back under the bridge and jumped up on the sofa it had shared with Stoutland. It wouldn't even look at Ash and the others.

"Litten . . ." Ash said, but Litten ignored him. It was clear the Pokémon wanted to be left alone.

Ash wasn't sure what to do. When it stopped raining, he decided to visit Litten's friend in the market. The shop lady gave Ash a lovely bag of Berries.

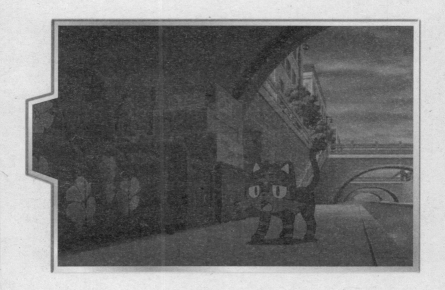

"Please take these to our friend," she said.

"I sure will. I hope these will cheer Litten up," Ash replied. He went to find Litten right away.

"Bet you're hungry. It's from the lady in the shop. She said you can come by anytime," Ash told Litten.

"Pikachu," Pikachu confirmed.

Most of all, Ash, Pikachu, and the others wanted Litten to know it could come to them. They wanted Litten to know that they cared.

It rained a lot over the next few days. Ash

thought about Litten all the time: during classes at the Pokémon School; during long walks in the rain; at dinner.

Litten had another visitor during those long, sad days, an unexpected visitor: Meowth.

"You can talk to me anytime, you know," Meowth told Litten. "See, sometimes talking things out can really help."

But even Meowth could not get Litten to talk.

Ash was worried about the stubborn young Pokémon. It hadn't eaten in days!

Ash decided that he could be stubborn, too. He came up with a plan.

"Litten?" Ash said the next time he went to visit. "We're going to hang out here until you decide to eat."

"*Pika,*" Pikachu agreed. It could be very stubborn, too.

"Professor Kukui said it was all right, so you're stuck with us," Ash explained. Then he sat down and offered Litten a Berry.

Meowth had been hiding in the shadows.

When he heard Ash's plan, he was impressed. "Crazy twerp," Meowth murmured.

Ash and his crew stayed that whole day, and they stayed the whole night.

The next morning, the rain had stopped. When Litten woke up, it heard something rustle nearby. When it went to see what it was, Litten noticed an amazing rainbow reaching across the sky—the colors were so pure and bright.

Then, just behind the rainbow, a cloud seemed to change shape. When Litten looked closely, it could see the face of Stoutland in the cloud! Stoutland seemed to be looking down at Litten with a kind, reassuring expression.

Ash and Pikachu came over to see what Litten was up to.

Something changed for Litten in that moment. It took one last look at the cloud before it changed shape again. Then, the Fire Cat Pokémon ran to the bag of fruit that Ash had brought. It grabbed a Berry, carried it over, and placed it in front of Ash.

"For me?" Ash questioned. "I think you should go on and eat first." He pushed the fruit in front of Litten.

"*Raaa,*" Litten grunted as it pushed the Berry back in front of Ash.

"No, really," Ash insisted, shoving the Berry again.

"*Raaa, raaa.*" Litten was as stubborn as always, and it wanted Ash to eat the Berry.

Ash placed the Berry back in front of Litten.

Back and forth.

Back and forth.

Back and forth.

"Pi-ka-chu!" Pikachu fell backward, nearly fainting with frustration! Why wouldn't either Ash or Litten give in?

Both Ash and Litten looked at Pikachu, and then at each other. Then they laughed.

"Hey, Litten," Ash said, kneeling down so he was eye level with the Pokémon, "do you want to join up with us?"

"Pika, pika!" Pikachu cheered. Now *this* was getting exciting!

"I think it would be awesome if you finished up your Fire Fang training with me!" Ash said hopefully. "You could be part of the family."

Litten looked uncertain. Then it squinted and shot an Ember move right at Ash's face.

"What?" Ash rushed over to the canal and dunked his head to put out the flames.

Up above on the bridge, Meowth had been observing. "I can dig that!" he commented. "First, Litten wants to battle. It wants no pity coming from a twerp."

Ash stood up and wiped his face off with his sleeve. "You want to battle?" Ash asked Litten. "What do you say?"

Pikachu bounded to Ash's side. Litten took battle position.

"Okay, but get ready for us," Ash warned. "Pikachu, use Thunderbolt!"

Pikachu lashed a Thunderbolt right at Litten, followed by Quick Attack. Litten fought back with Ember. The two Pokémon battled evenly, swapping attacks back and forth.

"Now Quick Attack!" Ash called, and Pikachu prepared its move.

"Litten is about to attack!" Rotom Dex said, but Ash directed Pikachu to counter with Iron Tail. The move's force slammed Litten against the wall.

"All right, use Quick Attack!" ordered Ash. "Electro Ball!"

Pikachu and Litten clashed in a smoky cloud and landed facing each other. The two were obviously well matched!

"So, you with us?" Ash asked their opponent. "Yeah?"

A sly smile crossed Litten's face.

"Then, go Poké Ball!" Ash yelled, holding the ball high in the air. "I just caught . . . a Litten!"

"I know it's for the best, Litten," Meowth sighed from where he had been watching on the bridge. "From now on, you're the enemy. So watch your twerpish back!"

"Litten, come on out!" Ash called, and the

feisty black-and-red Pokémon reappeared. "I'm glad you're coming along for the ride."

"*Raaa-raaa.*" Litten seemed happy, too.

"Now, how about we all eat together?" Ash suggested.

That was an idea the whole crew could agree on. Ash, Litten, Pikachu, Rotom Dex, Rowlet, and Rockruff all headed back to Professor Kukui's house . . . together.

CHAPTER 8

O kay, give it all you've got! Ready? Let's go!"
Ash was cheering on Litten. They were
on the beach, and the newest member of Ash's
team was practicing its Fire-type moves,
especially Fire Fang. Fire Fang was the attack
that Litten had been working on with Stoutland
for so long.

Rowlet, Rockruff, and Pikachu were all
watching and rooting for Litten, too.

"Litten's temperature is rising fast!" Rotom
Dex reported.

"Get ready to take whatever Litten dishes
out," Kiawe advised Turtonator. Of all Ash's
friends from the Pokémon School, Kiawe was
definitely the Fire-type expert. He'd agreed to
help Ash train Litten.

"You're doing great," Ash told the newest Pokémon on his team. "Go! Use Fire Fang!"

Litten pounced. It soared through the air, its entire body glowing a bright orange. Fire sprouted from its mouth. But just as it reached Turtonator's tail, the fire went out. Litten chomped down, but its jaws did not have any effect.

Rowlet and Rockruff ran forward to make Litten feel better. "You almost got it, you know,"

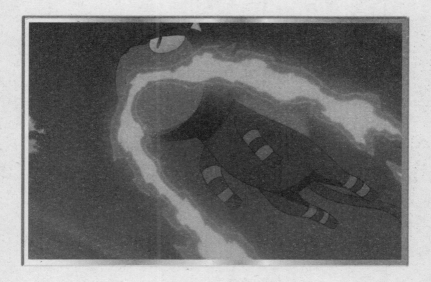

Ash said, kneeling down. "Kiawe and the gang can help you make all your moves great."

"All things Fire-type, leave it to me," Kiawe called.

Turtonator and Charizard agreed.

"Okay, let's try that again!" Ash said.

"Turtonator, use Flamethrower!" Kiawe called.

"You need to breathe deeply, just like Turtonator does," Rotom directed. "Do that, and your internal fire power will get stronger and stronger!"

"Okay, Litten, why don't you give it a try?" Ash said.

Litten arched its spine, and a spine of fire rose out of its back.

"Now, attack!" Ash yelled.

Litten sprang forward, gaining speed and power, but then it tripped on a piece of litter on the beach. "Pretty good. You'll get it next time," Ash promised.

Then Rockruff's joyful barks and Pikachu's happy coo distracted him. "What are they up to?" Ash asked.

"I think they're playing," Rotom Dex responded, watching the two Pokémon follow the handle of a shovel as it moved through the sand.

"Wait a sec! That shovel . . ." Kiawe said thoughtfully. "It's a Sandygast!"

"A Sandygast?" Ash questioned.

At that moment, the sand under the shovel began to rise. It grew into what looked like a sand ghost, with the shovel as its hat. Litten hissed.

"If you'll allow me . . ." Rotom Dex began. "Sandygast. The Sand Heap Pokémon. A Ghost-Ground-type. Sandygast can control people or Pokémon if they touch its shovel."

"Control?" Ash repeated.

"That's right," Kiawe confirmed. "Watch out, it's the most dangerous Pokémon on the beach.

My grandfather was constantly warning me when I was little. He'd say, 'Be careful around any shovel that looks like it's stuck in the sand at the beach. Something terrible could happen if you touch it.' But I was too curious and touched it once. Apparently I was gathering up sand until the next morning—in a complete daze."

"But it's just sand . . ." Ash responded, uncertain what to make of Kiawe's warning.

"Rock-ruff, ruff ruff. Rock-ruff." Sandygast made Rockruff nervous.

"Look out!" Kiawe called as Sandygast rose up and faced Rockruff.

"Rockruff! Use Rock Throw!" Ash directed.

Rockruff aimed and sent a blast of Rock Throw at Sandygast. The move knocked the shovel right off its head and into the ocean.

"It's really mad!" Ash cried as Sandygast growled and grew even taller. It shot Shadow Balls from its gaping mouth.

"Probably because it lost its shovel!" Kiawe pointed out.

"But it got knocked into the ocean, right?" Ash said.

"Then we have to go look for it!" Kiawe insisted. Without that shovel, they would not be able to set things right.

"Wait, Kiawe! I think the shovel can be replaced with something else," Rotom Dex suggested.

"But even if that's true, the shovel's what it wants," Ash said. Then he paused. "I've got an idea." Ash reached over and took the floating Rotom Dex in his hands.

"What? No-no-NO! What are you doing?!" Rotom Dex shouted.

"Ash . . . Are you serious?!" Kiawe asked.

"Just be a shovel for a little bit," Ash said to Rotom Dex.

"A shovel?! You're kidding!" Rotom Dex begged Ash to stop.

"Relax! It'll just be for a little while," Ash insisted as he approached the Sand Heap Pokémon.

"Wait! Whoa-whoa-whoa-WHOA!!" Rotom Dex screeched as Ash turned him upside down and inserted him into the sandy top of the Sandygast.

"This is so embarrassing," Rotom Dex mumbled.

"That's gonna work perfectly!" Ash said, satisfied.

But then Sandygast started to scowl . . . and growl.

"San-san-sandy-GAST!"

CHAPTER 9

What's going on?!" asked Rotom Dex as the unhappy Sandygast began to heave and grow. It was evolving!

"It looks different now," Ash commented. The heap of sand had turned into something that looked like a sand castle—a much larger sand castle.

"Hey, let me GO!" yelled Rotom Dex.

"Everyone, back off!" Kiawe directed, trying to keep them safe.

The Pokémon shivered and quaked, and then it grew even bigger—larger than a house!

"Ash!" Kiawe cried over the wind.

"Rotom!" Ash called out. "That's enough! Get away!"

Rotom Dex tried to pull itself out, but it couldn't move. "I'm stuck!"

"You're WHAT?!" Ash yelled.

"Ash, look out!" Kiawe warned. Ash was far too close to Sandygast. Suddenly, the outraged Pokémon folded over . . . and buried Ash!

"Ash!" Kiawe called.

"Pika, pika?" Pikachu was worried.

When the sand settled, the sand castle was massive, and Ash was inside!

"You okay?!" Kiawe checked.

"I'm fine!" Ash yelled from a window high up in the sand castle. "Is this a Pokémon? Or is it something else?"

"It's the evolved form of Sandygast: Palossand!" Rotom Dex explained. It was still stuck into the top of the now-enormous Pokémon. "The Sand Castle Pokémon. A Ghost- and Ground-type. It is said the shovel on Palossand's head functions as a radar."

"So I'm inside Palossand's body?" Ash asked. As he spoke, he lost his footing and slid all the way down to a lower level. "What's up with this thing?" he wondered, looking around. He ran up toward the window again and grabbed on.

Pikachu didn't like Palossand one bit. It started to zap the Pokémon's oversize body.

"Stop it, Pikachu!" Ash demanded, sliding back down again. "If you keep that up, I'll get zapped, too, and then I won't be able to move!"

Frustrated, Pikachu stopped its attack.

"Ash, are you having trouble getting out of there?" Kiawe called.

"I keep slipping back down because of the sand!" Ash explained. "We've gotta find that shovel, and fast!"

"Of course," Kiawe murmured. "Though the shovel's gone because of what you did . . ."

Ash and Kiawe's other classmates had hurried down the beach to see what was going on. "What's *that*?!" Lana asked with wonder and worry.

"Rrrrrr." At that moment, Rockruff raced forward and started barking at Palossand.

"Rockruff! That's dangerous!" Rotom Dex warned.

Litten ran up and pushed Rockruff out of the way. Just then, Palossand bent forward and covered Litten. When the huge Pokémon stood up again, Litten had disappeared!

"Litten!" Ash yelled.

Suddenly, Litten appeared in the same room as its Trainer. The Pokémon was in a heap on the sandy floor, and something wasn't right. Litten was glowing green.

"Litten?" Ash ran to its side.

Outside, on the Palossand's head, something similar was happening to Rotom Dex. "Hey . . . I . . . feel . . . strange . . ."

"Kiawe, is that a Pokémon?!" Mallow asked as she joined the others.

Kiawe filled them all in on what had happened.

"Ash, can you hear me?!" Mallow asked.

"Guys, something's wrong with Litten!" Ash told his friends.

"Ash, something's wrong with Rotom Dex, too!" Kiawe informed him. At the top of Palossand, Rotom was glowing a bright lime green.

"Somebody help me! Help!" Rotom squealed. Its voice was high and shaky. "I feel so strange."

"I read about this once," Lillie explained. "Palossand is most likely absorbing as much of

Rotom's and Litten's energy as it can in order to maintain its massive size!"

"Palossand's so big, it can even swallow a house!" Kiawe observed. "But we can't let it escape until we can help our friends!"

"Water washes sand away," Lana said hopefully. "Popplio, use Bubble Beam!"

At first, the attack seemed to be working, but then Palossand seemed to be fighting it off.

"Please stop that," Rotom called out. "Water-type moves will make Palossand even stronger!"

"This is serious," Mallow admitted.

"Palossand's looking for the shovel that should be on its head!" Kiawe pointed out. Then he told everyone about how the Pokémon's special shovel ended up in the ocean.

"We can't search the whole ocean!" Sophocles pointed out.

"Hold on," Lana said. "Popplio can find it."

"But," Kiawe advised, "if it touches the

shovel, Palossand will control it. Then Popplio will be lost!"

"But Popplio can make a balloon," Lana pointed out.

"Of course!" Kiawe cried. "That's it! Popplio can wrap the shovel in a balloon!" Kiawe was relieved that they finally had a good plan.

Now it was time to get to work.

CHAPTER 10

As Popplio prepared to enter the ocean, Pikachu trotted forward.

"Pika, Pikachu!" It wanted to help, and Popplio thought that was a great idea. Popplio nodded and started to blow a big balloon around the Mouse Pokémon. Then the two headed for the water.

"Good luck!" the classmates all cheered.

"They're off on a shovel search!" Lana called out.

"Great, buddy! I *know* you'll find that shovel," Ash yelled from inside Palossand. He turned to Litten. "You've got to hold on."

On the beach below, everyone was trying to figure out how to hold off Palossand. "If

Water-type moves aren't effective . . ." Kiawe thought aloud.

"Then maybe Snowy's Ice-type moves *will* be," Lillie suggested.

Lillie was still new to battling with Snowy. The Alolan Vulpix had hatched very recently, but Snowy was up to the challenge! "Here we go. We'll freeze Palossand using Powder Snow to stop it in its tracks," she said.

The friends just hoped it would keep Palossand from growing more powerful. They

didn't know how long it would take for Popplio and Pikachu to locate the shovel.

"All right," Kiawe announced. "We'll attract its attention. Then Snowy can use Powder Snow unnoticed."

The only concern was that Ash, Litten, and Rotom would get hit with Powder Snow, too. "Don't worry about us," Ash said. "Give it everything you've got!"

"Now, Snowy, let's go," said Lillie. She led Snowy, Lana, Mallow, Sophocles, and their partners to the other side of the beach. They would attack Palossand from the back. At the same time, Kiawe would command Charizard, Turtonator, Rockruff, and Rowlet to blast Palossand from the front.

"Sophocles and I are going to back up Snowy all the way!" Mallow declared. Togedemaru and Steenee agreed.

"Count on us!" Sophocles cried.

As soon as they were in position, Lillie gave

Snowy the go-ahead. "It's time, Snowy!" she directed. "You can do it!"

Inside Palossand, Ash reassured Litten. "We'll be out of here soon. And you'll be feeling much better in no time." Ash tucked Litten inside his shirt to help keep the Fire Cat Pokémon warm.

The teams continued with their two-sided battle. Snowy was working especially hard. It aimed blow after blow of Powder Snow.

"It's too much for Snowy," Lillie worried.

"That's why we're going to help out," Mallow said. She grabbed a giant palm leaf and started fanning behind Snowy, sending more waves of cold air at Palossand. When that seemed to be working, Lana and Sophocles joined in with leaves of their own. Steenee even waved with its long ears—and Lillie waved with her wide-brimmed hat!

"That's great! Keep it up!" Mallow called. "And one! And two! And three! And four!"

Meanwhile, Popplio and Pikachu were still searching for the missing shovel. It was hard to find on the colorful ocean floor.

"It looks like Palossand's finally starting to slow down!" Lillie announced.

"So it's working," Sophocles said, fanning even harder.

"Not much longer, Snowy!" Lillie called.

After a few more blasts, Palossand was completely frozen. All the classmates cheered and thanked their Pokémon partners.

"Oh, Snowy," Lillie whispered as she cuddled her Pokémon. "Thank you."

The next step was to rescue Ash, Litten, and Rotom Dex. Rowlet immediately took off to alert Ash that it was safe to try to make his escape.

"Rowlet, yes!" Ash said, cradling Litten in his arms. "Let's go."

Ash ran as hard as he could up the frozen slope of Palossand's insides. He made it to the window, but he couldn't get out of the frozen frame. He hit his head and slipped all the way back down.

Litten was no longer glowing green like a lime. Instead, it was glowing red like a flame. Litten was getting ready for an attack!

With a giant leap, Litten soared through the air. Fire burst from its mouth as it struck the ice on the window and destroyed it.

"Litten! You did it! You used Fire Fang!" Ash celebrated.

Litten beamed with success as Ash raced up

to the window so Kiawe's Charizard could fly over and pick them up.

"Hey, you guys!" Ash called out. His classmates were all relieved to see him and Litten safe.

Once he was securely on the Flame Pokémon's back, Ash asked Charizard to swing by so they could rescue Rotom Dex, too.

"Ash, be careful!" Mallow warned from below.

Ash and Litten jumped off Charizard's back. "Great job hanging in there, Rotom!" Ash said. "Litten, use Ember to melt the ice Rotom's stuck in," he directed.

But before Litten could focus its attack, Palossand woke up and started to quake underneath them. The Sand Castle Pokémon was as angry as ever!

"Where's that shovel?" Kiawe wondered, looking out at the ocean.

"There it is!" Lana called out.

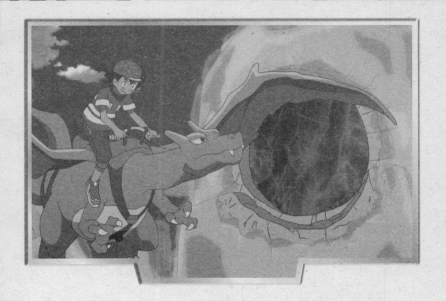

In the distance, a bubble burst out of the water—with a tiny toy shovel inside! Next, Pikachu appeared in a separate bubble. And last, Popplio popped out of the water.

"Awesome, Pikachu! You found it!" Ash yelled as he tried to free Rotom.

Together, the Pokémon batted the shovel-bubble toward Palossand. Popplio bobbed it in the air with its nose. Pikachu hit it with its tail.

Rockruff, Steenee, Togedemaru, and Rowlet all took turns tossing the bubble up high.

At last, when the shovel-bubble was directly overhead, Litten used Ember, popping the bubble so it fell straight down on Palossand's head.

At the exact same moment, Ash tugged on Rotom with all his might. "You're free!" Ash cried. But he lost his balance and started to tumble.

"Charizard!" Kiawe yelled. With a mighty swoop, the Flame Pokémon caught Ash, Litten, and Rotom in midair.

As soon as the shovel fell into place on Palossand's head, the mighty Sand Castle Pokémon shrunk back down to Sandygast, and then to just a tiny pile of sand with a shovel handle sticking out.

Once he and his Pokémon were safely on the ground, Ash looked around. "Oh, man. Sorry

about that," he said. He felt so lucky that his friends had teamed up to save him. They had all taken part and contributed. Even Snowy and Lillie, the newest partners, had been amazing! And Litten had mastered Fire Fang!

Ash could hardly believe how much he had learned from his classmates at the Pokémon School. What would the next step of his Alolan adventure bring?

Pokémon

Journey to the Orange Islands

SCHOLASTIC

Pokémon

Secret of the Pink Pokémon

SCHOLASTIC

Pokémon

The Four-Star Challenge

SCHOLASTIC

Pokémon

Scyther, Heart of a Champion

SCHOLASTIC

Pokémon

Talent Showdown

SCHOLASTIC

Pokémon

Race to Danger

SCHOLASTIC

Pokémon

Psyduck Ducks Out

SCHOLASTIC

Pokémon

Thundershock in Pummelo Stadium

SCHOLASTIC